TABLE OF CONTENTS

Title Page

Copyright

Contents

Dedication

Dr. Frank Stein

Sleep Paralysis

Bone Record

Sirens

Player 2 Has Entered The Game

Batteries Not Included

Waters Blue

Baptized

Happy Hunting

Obituary Killer

Human

It's time

Bug Repellent

We Interrupt Your Regular Program

Till Death Do You Part

The Clown

You're It

Newborn

Dante's Descent

- [Chapter 1](#)
- [Chapter 2](#)
- [Chapter 3](#)
- [Lord of the Dead Flies](#)
  - [Day 1: Morning](#)
  - [Day 1: Midnight](#)
  - [Day 1: Breakfast](#)
  - [Day 2: Dawn](#)
  - [Day 1: Brunch](#)

HICCUP RELIEVERS

MARIO LAVALLE

Copyright © 2019 by Mario Lavalle

All rights reserved.

No part of this book may be reproduced in any form or by any electronic or mechanical means, including information storage and retrieval systems, without written permission from the author, except for the use of brief quotations in a book review.

Formatted by Fireproof Editing

CONTENTS

Dr. Frank Stein

Sleep Paralysis

Bone Record

Sirens

Player 2 Has Entered The Game

Batteries Not Included

Waters Blue

Baptized

Happy Hunting

Obituary Killer

Human

It's time

Bug Repellent

We Interrupt Your Regular Program

Till Death Do You Part

The Clown

You're It

Newborn

Dante's Descent

Chapter 1

Chapter 2

Chapter 3

Lord of the Dead Flies

Day 1: Morning

Day 1: Midnight

Day 1: Breakfast

Day 2: Dawn

Day 1: Brunch

I would like to dedicate this book to my father for showing me my very first horror movie, Night of the Living Dead, 1968, and to my Aunt Donna for showing me many, many others.

DR. FRANK STEIN

A young man's head sat on a table, eyes closed and lifeless as life intended, once a head was removed from a body but would soon be woken from its peaceful rest and brought back to this world. This world where a single bulb out of four shown bright down on the subject and the table beneath, while the other three were blown and coated with black dust. The Camera was recording and the little red light flashed like a blood lit metronome showing other dead things in the back, strung up like animals but in this world of taboo barriers were only broken down by trailblazers. By being the 1st to dive involved certain risks or ridicules, but when mankind will be able to live forever they will forget about the cracked eggs that screamed in agony and savor the taste of the omelet, sweet, and life.

The silent generator started to rumble at the yank of the pull cord and the cables running from the generator to the head on the table also brought electricity. The heads' eyes began to twitch and his mouth went crooked causing a slow flow of saliva to drip down from the corners of his mouth, while clicking or smacking sounds could be heard. The throat twitched and spasmed, as if the brain was telling him to breathe, but there were no lungs to inhale or exhale oxygen.

"Do you remember how you died?" asked Dr. Frank Stein sitting out of camera's view.

The head clicked up and down in quick rhythmic spasms, while his eyes never stopped looking around, as if it's searching for his body.

"Do you know who I am?" Asked the Doctor, after finishing his notes, again the young man's chin jumped up and down, but this time, his mouth moved and a voice came out, a voice that seemed to have been punched in the stomach if it had one.

"Fa-ther"

SLEEP PARALYSIS

It was a dreamless sleep until it no longer was. The man woke up, not in the middle, but at the very beginning of a nightmare. He lay there, looking through fluttering eyes as if he was in a room with a strobe light. Movement or any function besides breathing and seeing had left him, and paralysis came to visit. The walls were clean of any memorabilia or family photos, but now, there was a wooden cross, like the kind you would find in a cathedral from the times of Beethoven and Mozart, with intricate wood carvings. It wasn't the cross that startled Jeremy, but what the cross started to do. With every flutter of the eye, the cross slid smoothly against the wall like the big hand on a clock until it was completely upside down. What was already dark in an unlit room was now darker as if a passing cloud had come through the window.

He tried to scream, but all that came out was a moan of despair. It was a loud moan for anyone to hear and rescue him. Jeremy started to slide down the bed as if some hands held him by his ankles but he felt no such thing, just sheets beneath him crumpling and pulling back at his shorts and shirt. There was nothing he could do except grab onto passing sheets and hold on as long as he could, but he was still being pulled by phantom hands. All Jeremy could think to do was pray to any righteous deity who would listen, but he just kept being pulled down, onto the ground, prayers unanswered, and pulled under the bed.

BONE RECORD

The House had been off the market for decades and when they had purchased it, it was at an auction and the seller was in the city. They had gutted out the entire house and the attic was last on the list. The Robinsons were minimalists that never really celebrated the holidays, so there was no need for storage or anything really except major appliances. Mark was on attic duty while his wife Misty would finish up the downstairs. The staircase went up to an old faded red door that seemed out of place even for the time it was built or any other owner that had it since. Every step closer the colder it got, and by the time he had reached the knob, his arms were covered in goosebumps in the middle of July. The door only opened to another staircase that went up another handful of steps and Mark's inner child wanted to run back down and forget they even have an attic, but eventually, they would sell, while he would have to come back to the attic to clear it out, so he might as well get it out of the way.

Mark didn't see much of anything except old floorboards, a table under a windowsill, and a couple of old shelves that made aisle like rows with boxes scattered throughout like cubed land mines that were placed randomly with no rhyme or reason; so, he decided to look into a random box and found some old whiskey glasses surrounded by old napkins that almost crumbled under his touch. Now, things were turning around, but the glasses would be the only thing worth anything, the rest were trinkets and knick knacks unless you counted cob webs, then Mark would never have to work again. He continued to walk towards the back to see what was sitting above everything else and not only was it on the shelf all alone in the corner of the house, it was as if objects were allergic to it, not even a cobweb, or a speck of dust.

Mark reached for it and pulled it down off the shelf and walked it over to the nearest table that sat under a windowsill. It was an old record player that was made of black cherry wood and brass accents that gleamed so clean it could pass for gold. A sleeve held a small record that was white instead of its standard black, with no label or artists name and seemed to be made out of some type of bones. The brass spoke sprouted from the back left corner like a golden cyclone that could fit a bowling ball at its widest circumference. He reached for the disc to further inspect and It was a flat disc with smooth carvings, circled valleys that caught whatever light there was as if it was cut with diamonds. He looked for a cord to plug in but there wasn't a cord, he looked for a power button but there was no button.

Frustrated and confused, Mark picked it up and brought it downstairs to get a second opinion from his wife Misty, but she was nowhere to be found and their car was out of the driveway. He came back to it to examine it some more, and noticed some old English writing on the sleeve that he hadn't noticed earlier.

"Those who listen, hear your exit, some remain, some may change, but death will come, either way"

There were no initials or hint as to who wrote it, but someone had taken the time to write the poem. Mark continued to tinker with it until he lost interest and continued with his chores forgetting all about the portable record player. He was just getting out of the shower and dressed when he heard her scream like he had never heard her scream before. When he came down, the dull white record was spinning but there was no music or melody. He scanned the room looking for her, but she wasn't there or visible until he calmed down and stopped searching wildly. Misty sat facing the corner rocking back and forth on the cold tile floor, while cupping her ears shaking her head left to right, right to left like a child not wanting to listen.

When he bent down to pick her up and comfort her, a melody intended for Mark to hear echoed throughout their new home.

SIRENS

An old fishing boat carrying seven friends and competitors stopped in a new location hoping for their big catch. The night was especially dark and eerily foggy, but only on the surface of the water like oil refusing to mix. David was the new one to fishing or any outdoor activities, and David felt he would never get used to the sea most of all. Some men attended to their usual tasks and preparations, while two others popped open a beer before doing so. "It'd be safer for everyone if you just stay outta the way this time, just watch and learn. Go on top and hold the spotlight." Carl said and since Carl was the owner and Captain, David didn't have much of a choice.

David was above the deck looking down controlling the spot light, getting a bird's eye view of all the action, the men worked like machines, machines that were programmed to sail, catch, sail back, rinse and repeat. He was looking out into the water wondering when the fog let up and instead it seemed like a bunch of sparkling eyes were watching him but they were just the reflection of the stars on a black melting mirror. The ocean seemed to be competing with the sky but met somewhere on the horizon, split by two different shades of void. A hand was waving in the corner of Dave's eye, which wasn't coming from the starboard side deck, but the water.

The flesh was that of a fish, scaly and slick looking. The head was similar to that of a human but structured with points at the top of the head, like a crown with hair green as seaweed sprouting in between real human hair. Dave was lost in observation and eventually met with its eyes, eyes similar to a squid, big and black but with bright white polka dots scattered throughout like the stars that were reflecting off the water...or looking up at him. It showed no fear staring back directly into Dave's eyes, and when it smiled, it revealed teeth like that of a piranha, short, sharp triangles that looked as though they were anticipating something. As Dave was losing grips on reality, so was he on the deck light duties.

"HEY GREENHORN, SHINE THE LIGHT OVA HERE YA MORON!" Shouted Rick while everyone else on deck snickered, "USUALLY YOU WANT TO SHINE THE LIGHT ON THE ACTION NOT THE WATER!" finished Rick while continuing his jokes with the rest of the crew in a lower tone.

Dave looked around the boat as if he had owl ancestry. Looking for any sign of the creature that waved but there was nothing, not even the stars seemed to have been reflecting off the water anymore. Then the nets that were being reeled in by the ropes and pulleys started seizing and locking up, and from the looks on everyone's faces, this wasn't an everyday occurrence. As the bag breached the surface David moved the captains light to get a better view of what was inside, but all anyone could see were fish. The giant bag hit the deck and like sand flattened out with fluttering fish tails smacking the deck except the middle of the bag. The middle was large and seemed to be moving with dramatic breaths being taken that sounded wheezy. The closest one to the closely knitted net revealed what was under and within a blink of an eye it screamed a high pitch tune that caused almost everyone's ears to bleed but did bring everyone to their knees, holding their heads while the glass and lights shattered all around them.

The deck hand with a bird's eye view also had the advantage of being behind the light, so his eyes didn't have to adjust as long as everyone else's and was able to see it and grabbed Rick by the leg. With its other scaly appendage, it reached for the rail for support and with inhuman strength lifted itself above the rail, slamming Ricks head to the deck, while spinning on its bottom and whipping its tail, hitting Glenn in the chest sending him overboard. In the seconds of mayhem, David saw the face of the creature and it wasn't the one in the water previously, but another one with a bigger face and broader shoulders that moved on deck as if it were below deck. David froze from the unbelievable sight as if he wasn't able to comprehend what he had just seen. The men that were closest to Rick and Glenn stood up to run back inside, but were met with obstacles.

A spear made of a stingray barb, attached to some interwoven seaweed sprouted from the water and into Ryan's chest. Before he was even able to fall in pain he was yanked backward, hitting his back against the rail and wincing once more reaching out to any of the four left, including David. Ryan's eyes met with everyone and no one, before he could let out a plea, the medieval looking weapon was yanked once more to bring the next victim overboard. David once relieved of his trance started to search the waters wildly looking every which way for a trace of his co-worker and there was, a yellow raincoat floating, empty of any person. "OVER THERE!" David shouted, pointing out at the water. Carl and Justin both reluctantly followed David's finger to the coat and decided in unison to run inside, all except David.

Hoping to catch a glimpse of Rick surfacing was diminished when the same scaly hand reached up and over the coat as if forgotten memorabilia, and that's when David decided it was time to follow the rest of the crew. Before David could leave, a twinkle hit the corner of his eye and when he turned he saw the original creature, but this time blood trailed from the corners of its mouth and like a light switch all the stars glittered on the surface once more. It waved the same, slow swaying wave as if imitating a first encounter it had with a human but it wasn't a salutation the way this creature did it. This time, David didn't stick around to further observe, but went downstairs to find the last three companions he had left.

"Ryan, Glenn, and Rick are GONE!" Justin said still in shock

"What could chuck a spear from the water?" Carl asked, hoping for a reasonable explanation.

"It's some type of hybrids, a Siren" added Howard

"What's a Siren?" asked Justin

"Mermaid" Answered Carl, "I heard a story once, but that's all I took it for - a story."

David interrupted "What happened in the story?"

Carl sat with his hands covering his face, taking a deep breath before telling the tall tale. "There was a small charter boat that went out for some night fishing, with a handful of passengers but only one came back." The captain said making it short and sweet, sparing his crew the gruesome details.

"Well, how did he survive?" Justin asked.

"The story says, if to be believed, he jumped in willingly."

The room went silent from hearing the end of the story and coming to the conclusion that it would be suicide to imitate. But by the time they went, the job was already done, and that's when they heard the slick, flopping tentacles came into focus instead of Carl's voice, the same interwoven seaweed rope that yanked Ryan over was being wrapped around Carl's leg by a camouflaged octopus, as if a seal on a recon mission. One of the most intelligent sea inhabitants tugged at the rope and after a few moments of everyone putting two and two together, David leaped for Carl, but he flew over him as the rope yanked him down so viciously the back of his head cracked open on the floor making a thud sound that sounded like death. Justin and Howard stood in paralysis, while the octopus hitched a ride atop of Carl, leaving a red snail trail that would undoubtedly stop at the rails and point towards the water.

"We have to hide," Justin said.

"Hide where? That octopus just came in here without being seen and was able to take Carl. Where do we hide?" David replied.

"We leave then." Spat out Justin, shooting ideas from the hip.

"Do you know how to drive a boat?" David asked.

"Do you think that'll stop me?" Justin asked, letting his anger and other emotions get the best of him.

"We have to be smart about this and keep calm. What happens if we get caught in a storm? We could end up in the water. A wave bigger than usual and you turn the wrong way; we end up in the water."

"That's a chance I'm willing to take," Justin snapped back with the intent behind the words. He would not be stopped from trying, and would do whatever necessary out in the open waters to survive.

"Are you not hearing me? A mistake could get us all killed!" David said, ready to fight, clinching his fists and stepping in front of the steering wheel.

"Guys, I could do it," Howard said softly to himself, not really sure if he could, but he's seen Carl do it enough, which was more than the other two combined.

"You honestly think you could beat me up?" Justin said, smirking once he noticed David's clinched fists.

"Do you think that'll stop me?" David asked, giving Justin his own words to eat on.

"Guys, I could do it." Howard said, a bit louder.

"Well, we're about to find out the green horn." Justin said, while taking off his rain coat.

"Hope you know how to swim?" David replied, while taking his coat off as well.

"GUYS, I CAN GET US HOME!" Screamed Howard, finally cutting through the tension and tunnel vision his companions had.

They both stopped to hear the same sounds prior to Carl's demise, but this time, David reacted quick enough and bear hugged Howard, while Justin seemed to catch paralysis. The yank sent them both to the ground almost knocking out the both of them but David was lucky or hard headed because he came back from the haze of pain and reached for Carl while his other hand kept a hold of the dining tables leg. When the second yank came, Justin finally came to and jumped down on Carl to help and it did until the 3rd yank. The 3rd yank ripped Howard away from his shoulder, while David and Justin still held onto Howard's arm. His screams echoed until they reached the open deck and continued until they were seized by a splash of water.

"You just killed us." Justin said, wanting to put the blame on someone else.

David's eyes flashed with anger and he moved towards Justin to settle it once and for all, but he lost his balance and rolled with gravity. When the boat rocked hard to one side, the momentum sent it back the other way just as much, like a pendulum. The boat rocked hard to starboard side and they both looked at each other, knowing what they were up to. Rocking from one side to the other more and more, the momentum would eventually capsize the boat, and then, there would be nowhere to hide. Justin lost his grips on the dining table, and lost against gravity, falling about 15 feet to crash through the window and into the water. Once they received their latest victim, the boat stopped rocking and came to its natural sway.

Everything seems to be normal, the usual wave coming and going partnered with the wind, the rocking, creaking wood that spoke of emptiness, and the water to come in through the crashed window washed away the blood and the evidence of anyone ever being aboard. David walked out into the open where the moon was leaving and the stars already left, the sea was calm as if in the middle of a lake and David's sense of security sunk to the bottom of his boots when the reflection of the stars all returned staring up at him once more, and in the distance the original Siren floating, waving a welcoming, menacing slow wave, but there was nothing welcoming about it and the boat began to rock once more.

PLAYER 2 HAS ENTERED THE GAME

A boy walked into his bedroom where he heard familiar sounds, but there was no one at home. His TV was on and the game was in the middle of its pre-menu video, but as it played on, he convinced himself that maybe he had left it on before he went to play outside. It was something he had done before which got him in trouble; so, it was possible for him to make the mistake, but not likely because the light was off. He entered the room and turned the light on, picking up the first-player controller while sitting on the bed and getting in his usual position of lying belly down with his face at the end of the bed closest to the TV, while the second-player's controller sat on the floor from the last time his friend was over playing with him.

The boy picked his favorite fighter and selected his opponent at random. He sat, waiting for the game to load and when it did, he was prepared with a set of combos to unleash on the computer's chosen character, but before contact was made, the screen flashed and the print read "player 2 enters the game."

The boy sat in amazement and fear, not knowing what to think of this, and the game continued as if someone really was playing, going to the character selection menu and actually picking out a character to combat with. Again, he allowed it to play on, wondering if the glitch would eventually play itself out, but instead, it continued to play.

Round one started, and the boy fought as if he would any person or A.I., but he could hear clicks matching player two's movements, so he looked down at the second controller to see the buttons moving, being pressed by phantom fingers, fighting a frozen player one. The boy stood up to turn the game off and to run back outside, but before he could jump off the bed, his bedroom door closed and the lights turned out.

BATTERIES NOT INCLUDED

Today, Katie's daughter Ashley was turning seven. Between errands, raising a child by herself and working almost fifty hours a week at minimum wage, it made it harder for her to lavish her daughter with pretty things and expensive gifts, but this was something she had purchased for next to nothing. In fact, it was practically given to her.

Katie had stopped on the way home from work at a church yard sale. It was sloppy and scattered with broken antiques, retro board games, and dolls that seemed to be made by children, but the item that caught her eye was a teddy bear sitting at a table all by itself. With all of its character flaws, it still would be better than no gift at all, and even when used, it still was in its original packaging. Katie took it out to further examine this teddy bear she would take home and it was as white as snow, where it was clean and other spots where dark stains cluttered from a spill or splatter of some sorts, Katie shrugged it off to old age and food stains. The bear's eyes sparkled like black diamonds.

It was a battery-powered stuffed animal that still had its batteries, but when she pressed the paw of the bear, all that came out were distorted slow rumblings, incoherent sounds that might scare a child, so Katie figured she would buy some batteries on the way home. Katie put the bear back into the box, closed it up and looked around for someone to haggle with, since there was no tag or sticker on it. The few employees the church had were busy breaking down all the items that were left over to be sold another day, so Katie dipped into her wallet to pull out a few bucks and walked over to the nearest person to corner them with cash in hand.

"I would like to buy this teddy, please," Katie said holding out the premeditated bargain of three dollars to be grabbed and to finalize the transaction, but when the employee turned around, he jumped rearing his head back as if a bee buzzed by. "I'm sorry I didn't mean to scare you," Katie said with all sincerity. "I just wanted to buy this teddy bear."

The man's eyes were fixed on the bear's without ever even noticing the lady holding it. "No money necessary; it's all yours," and before she even had the chance to say thank you or force the three dollars on him, he turned and walked away to complete his tasks. Katie shrugged and got back into her car and tossed the box in the back seat. She stopped at the gas station to buy batteries and to fill up, but after she put the hose back and got back into her car, the box was in the passenger seat with the teddy facing her. Katie didn't jump or scream; she just stared back, second-guessing herself, not knowing if she had placed it there or tossed it in the back because all the other scenarios were madness.

The widowed mother grabbed the batteries and the bear to enter the house, but within the turn of the key, Ashley was being dropped off by the school bus and running up the driveway.

"Hey, birthday girl. How old are we now?"

Ashley smiled, looking up at her mother with all five fingers sprawled out. "FIVE! Is that for me?" she asked already tugging at the teddy knowing the answer.

"Yes, you are five years old—a little lady. Well, Mommy didn't have time to wrap it, but she got you a teddy to keep you company in your new room, since you'll be sleeping in your new bedroom tonight."

The little girl's face was all smiles and both arms were out waiting to hug the very life out of the teddy bear, and that's what she did while running up the stairs.

"Don't stay up there too long; dinner's almost ready."

"OKAY," yelled Ashley from her newly decorated bedroom.

Katie put the bag with the batteries down on the entry dresser, not giving it another thought. Once dinner was ready and the table set, Katie yelled upstairs, "IT'S TIME TO EAT!" but all she heard were whispers: one voice was her daughter's and the other was that of deep rumbles. It sounded similar to the bear's voice. Katie walked closer to the staircase and on top of the entry dresser were the un-opened batteries still in the bag. Katie's heart sank and she wanted to run up the stairs and grab her daughter, but she didn't. She crept one step at a time trying to hear the conversation going on between her daughter and something else.

It was a crisp voice that came in through the old speakers, but before she reached the door, the voice went silent as if it knew someone was listening. Katie walked through the door to see the teddy on the windowsill staring deep into her daughter's eyes as she sat on the floor, smiling. When the teddy bear finally noticed Katie, it turned from the neck up robotically and what seemed to be an already massive smile now was gigantic from ear to ear.

"No Mommy. We want to keep playing, and you're going to play with us."

Ashley's little hand reached up from the floor and grabbed her mother's wrist with un-usual strength and brought her down to her knees.

The last of his boat was sinking and an opportunist had already arrived, smelling the blood flowing from a wound he had taken falling overboard. A large, dark-grey fin was slicing through the water off in the distance, and with every frightened heartbeat, more blood flowed from the wound. The distance between them was close to thirty feet and closing. And then fifteen, the man's blood was betraying him, and then ten feet. Then the fin submerged and disappeared from sight.

BAPTIZED

The congregation surrounded Father Dennis and the newcomer Ash to witness what was supposed to be a baptism, but instead, they witnessed much more. Father Dennis grabbed Ash with one hand cradling the back of his head and the other hand pushing him under the water, the clear, sparkling blessed water that seemed to be turning black. Black as oil but still light in consistency, and Father Dennis's grip released. As he took steps backward, Ash's eyes showed through the darkness and they were zeroed in on the priest. Ash, who was supposed to be cleansed and reborn rose instead became impure and evil incarnate, screams echoed throughout the building as stampeding feet ran to the door. The man walked over to Father Dennis and with both hands, he grabbed at the base of his jaw and yanked up so violently and fast that his entire spine followed like a piece of thread caught in a doorway. The stained glass windows no longer let the sun in and the doors clicked loudly, locking them in. Ash raised the priest's head above his own and began to drink the blood that ran down the severed spine. He smiled while looking at everyone. "Gulp" Knowing this was just the beginning... "Gulp"

HAPPY HUNTING

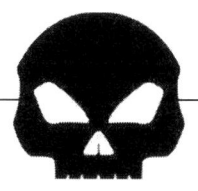

The charter was carrying about twenty people to a party island only known to a certain select few. As they were docking, they were met by a small crowd of what seemed to be hunters in the most theatrical way imaginable, but what they kept on chains were real: starved and crazy-eyed people who looked like they had rabies. The crowd walked slowly down the dock until what had been their captain let a round off behind them and in unison, all reacted in their own way.

"GET ONTO THE BEACH NOW!" the captain yelled, while still pointing the gun in the air. And when no one moved, he pointed the gun at no one in particular, then one by one, they all stood and continued down to what seemed to be a death row. As they gathered on the soft sand, one of the people holding a gun started to talk.

"This is Hunters' Island, and we are the hunters. These people you see chained up here are the lucky ones; they are our pets. The not-so-lucky ones look like this." And without a hint of warning, he lifted his pistol and shot some man in the throat. While everyone started screaming, the chained up "pets" went crazy and acted as if it was dinner time. The man who had been doing the talking and shooting walked over to one of his pets, unchained him, and like a real-life zombie, it started to eat the man alive. As everyone stared in horror, another shot went off and even the pet stopped biting. but never stopped chewing.

"Now that we are on the same page, here are the rules: Answer whatever questions we might have correctly and you may make it to the second round. Answer them incorrectly and die. For example," the man walked over to a frightened young man who was sobbing, "what is the chemical symbol for helium? You should know this, Keith." The young man looked up even more frightened that the gun-wielding psycho knew his name. "You have three seconds to answer," said the main hunter, raising his pistol to Keith's head.

"H.h.h.E.e," stuttered Keith.

"DING, DING, DING! You just hit a life raft bonus. Pick one individual to go with you and run into that forest behind us. The rest of you get ready for a pop quiz.

"Honey, have you read the obituary?" Gus inquired, with a tone his wife had never heard before.

As she was walking into the kitchen from the living room, she stopped in the doorway to see her husband staring down into the paper. "It says we've passed away tragically. Double hom..." A glass of water hit the kitchen floor before Gus could continue and startled he looked up from his paper to see his wife in the doorway looking behind him in absolute horror. A man with a burlap sack for a mask stood behind her husband flashing a serrated blade.

Jonathan and his new friend walked through double doors to almost a theater venue. The place was packed as if the Super Bowl was about to be screened but no such luck. The stage was empty and the room was quiet. There weren't any eyes on them, but he could swear he was being looked at through their peripherals. Once his new friend showed him to his seat and sat down as if a domino had been pushed a bright light hit the stage and a man walked out almost robotically and stopped in the center to turn not the audience but Jonathan. "Do you hear it?" Asked the man on stage, Jonathan didn't know if he should answer or not, or if it was even him he was talking to. Silence pursued until the man on the stage spoke once more. "His heartbeat deceives him. He is not one of us." They all stood up as if given a command even his new friend and all eyes were now undoubtedly on him.

IT'S TIME

A young boy walked into a dark hallway from his bedroom. He was going to meet his father in the living room, but he felt something walking along with him, not near him but at the other end of the hallway. It was a big home, with two stories and countless rooms; half of them had toilets in them. The boy looked and saw something resembling the Grim Reaper, but instead of black, there was a bright glittery red, as if stitched together with rubies, but it wasn't human. Where flesh should be, there was bone; where feet would touch hardwood floor, there was nothing but air and floating ruby red drapery. The boy froze not in horror but in awe. The thing turned and looked at the boy, stopping in mid-air, hovering. Its hood covered all features and the darkness helped conceal even the whiteness of the eyes, if there were any.

Not knowing whether to run or curl up into a ball, he simply stared back in almost a calm state, more inquisitive than frightened, but the entity made it easy on the boy and turned to continue on its path, which was on its way into the boy's grandparents' room, where his bed-ridden grandfather lay. The boy, not knowing what intentions it had, moved lightning quick to turn on the hallway light before the reaper entered its destination. As quick as the light came on, the bright ruby red cloak and hallowed face disappeared. The boy stood staring down the hallway not knowing what to believe. He turned the light out once more and nothing was there, like so many times before tonight, so he turned it on once more and finally back off to make double sure.

The boy carried on with the night not wanting to tell his father what he saw, fearing he would sound crazy. Instead, he talked of ghosts and beliefs. They weren't a church-going family, but they were believers of energy and of an after-life. Whether what the boy saw was good or bad, he would never know, at least not until the next morning.

The boy woke up to the usual routine of his father above him taking the blankets off and a gentle shake of the shoulder, but this morning, his father looked solemn.

"Your grandfather passed away last night."

BUG REPELLENT

The process of evolution is slow. It can take up to centuries to witness even the slightest of changes, some far less, some only thirty years. It's been documented some plants evolve in even a shorter time than that, so who's to say what Mother Nature will do when chemicals are brought into the equation? We will find out. A catalyst that will go unchecked until the next government official takes office and as usual per politician, he turns a blind eye. A chemical that had been tested with remarkable effects on killing bugs without any harm to the environment or man, until one day, it was very hazardous to mankind, almost genocidal.

The chemicals carried out through the food chain had little effect on the consumer but not the insects. The insects that didn't die were changing. They were growing to Goliath sizes, and because the secrecy of the chemicals and the location of the farm, no one asked any questions until a couple of scientists and known agriculturists were found ripped apart, but even then, why ask questions when a farm half the size of your average farm can yield crops like the top two do, combined?

The media did its part and reported on very little because there was a conflict of interest; so, after some years, people had forgotten and it became a bear mauling or something bigger had gotten hungry, but there weren't claw marks in the report or pictures. There were chunks of meat and bone missing, as if a hippo in the middle of farmland USA had been the culprit. These were truths people were happy to ignore because to question their reality would mean they would have to face it, and how could they come to terms with such a thing? They'd learn because those who didn't have died or something worse became of them. There are worse things than death, and it's how you meet that death. Some were eaten, some from the inside, some torn apart limb from limb being pulled every which way like first graders fighting over the only good toy during play time. This would be the world's new reality, and reality was stranger than fiction.

It was as if the human race reversed in time to the age of dinosaurs with the simplest of creatures reaching colossal sizes and appetites to match. The only things humans had on their side were science, data, and weapons, but the data previously recorded on certain species didn't account for a thousand times the normal size, and the weapons that were once powerful didn't hold up to a 17-foot tall arachnid or insect, and the ones that did kill, wouldn't kill without causing collateral damage. Even then, most insects were survivors of the harshest conditions, but the human race would survive also. It had to; it **has** to.

IF YOU FIND THIS LETTER, I am Detective Pervez. There isn't anything left here, and you need to head for Alcatraz Island. We need all the help we can get....

"What's wrong?"

"The letter just stops, and there's blood on it."

Clicks and churps sounded outside and the ground began to shake.

WE INTERRUPT YOUR REGULAR PROGRAM

A TV was playing in the background for white noise, while Andrew was cleaning his apartment. He had put it off for too long, and the trash was starting to become a tripping hazard. After a while of cleaning, he realized there was no sound coming from the living room, no commercial to be heard or jingle, not his show or theme music, just silence. When he entered the living room, the TV was on but there were four pale faces staring at Andrew, watching him. He grabbed the remote and changed the channel but no such luck; he hit the power button and again the same result. Four pale faces stared deep into Andrew's soul. He walked up to the TV to unplug it from the socket and right when he did, a deep voice from the speaker echoed out into his apartment.

"Don't..." and like that, the TV was cut off. Andrew, not wanting to further investigate or even acknowledge what had happened, turned on the radio to finish his cleaning and to prepare for his night out. Once everything was complete, he took a shower, and by then, he had forgotten what had happened just a couple of hours prior, but then the radio went silent. Andrew finished up in a hurry, wrapped the towel around his waist and ran out of the bathroom, down the hall and into the living room where he saw the TV had been turned back on, but the cord still lay on the floor. This time there were only three faces staring back at Andrew and in the corner of his eye, he saw a shadow move inside his apartment.

A man was with his date driving down a long windy road that seemed to never come to an end. Glowing streetlights gave no sight to anything important except more road. The song they were listening to had come to an end, and a familiar voice appeared through the speakers, not to his date but to him.

"She's not even the one you killed me for, David."

The lights in the vehicle started to dim and the engine sounded to skip and putter along until he pulled it over onto the shoulder where the car finally gave up and cut off. David tried turning the key multiple times, knowing there was gas in the tank, but the engine never turned. He started slamming on the steering wheel screaming in anger while his date started to get scared.

"What was that about, David? Who was that?" she asked with her back against the door.

"I don't know, maybe it was meant for another David," but his tone suggested he was lying, too frightened to put his full attention on her and the lie. "See if you have service on your phone. Mine's dead."

She gladly took the opportunity and stood out of the car holding her cell phone and dialing 911, but there wasn't any service.

"You get anything?" David asked.

"Not yet. I'm resetting my phone," she said, while turning to look down the never-ending road. A streetlight turned off, then another, and another, then another. She looked behind her and the same was happening. "David…"

He didn't answer. He couldn't answer after seeing what was going on in front of his eyes until the light above them was the only one on, and it started to flicker. Before David's date could reenter the vehicle, the light turned out and her screams were made of nightmares. Screams of pure pain and agony almost begging for death, but they could be heard everywhere. Above him, to the left of him, under the car, and then the light above him turned back on while his date and her screams had disappeared from the earth. David reached over, closing his missing date's door. He kept trying to start the car until the light flickered once more; he looked up to see his dead wife in the darkness only to vanish with the flicker of the light and reappear when the darkness took over.

The cops arrived the next morning, pulling up to an abandoned vehicle with the radio playing, but there was no one inside.

THE CLOWN

It was an eight-hour shift; he happened to be on the graveyard shift, the shift John Edward loved the most. It was only him and two other guys, so that meant there weren't too many eyes watching, and you could cut corners without getting too much gripe for it. There weren't any fellow laborers or mechanics screaming obscenities or telling vulgar jokes; it could be almost therapeutic working in the factory alone, just him, his tools, and his thoughts to keep him busy, which in turn made the shift go by much quicker, but that wasn't the case tonight. Tonight, Ted and Garth were a part of the rotating shift and made it near impossible for John to get any work done in the mill with all of the practical jokes going on. Why should he work any harder when Ted was bound to receive the credit? John had dealt with nepotism before, but Ted was literally a man-child playing game and disrupting work whenever he had the opportunity.

The occasional steam whistle would blow and mechanical sounds would echo throughout the factory, but this was a different sound, a sound John Edward only heard in movies or in his nightmares. It was a deep growl that rumbled the steel walkway underneath his feet. John's head moved like an owl twisting all the way around, searching wildly to see the source and hoping it was something that could be explained, but there was nothing, just another steam whistle blowing and more clanks of steel on steel from old turning grinds. This factory was old, and it was possible something had finally broken down, which would explain the vibration beneath his feet, but he was seasoned and this sound was nothing mechanical.

"TED!" John yelled out, hoping his fellow co-workers were there just playing the usual trick on him as they had with each other so many times before, but there was no answer, just another steam whistle and echoing clanks of steel on steel. Why would Ted give away the game when John knew his inquisition had a tone of fear in it? There wasn't much to do to pass the time except play tricks on one another, and this had to be a trick, something Ted was saving in his back pocket or up his sleeve, never revealing he was a man of sounds or impressions. John wished that was the only plausible explanation, but he would be brought back to reality, if this was a reality.

John finally was able to convince himself it was something else: a cat caught a rat, or something fell, making a sound never heard. When John was finally comfortable, the sound returned, echoing throughout the plant and vibrating his feet even more. John searched frantically as if his head was on a swivel looking left to right, up and…down. At the foot of the stairs beneath him through grated walkways, he caught a quick glimpse of shoes. They weren't factory-safe but bright red. John rubbed his eyes to make sure he was seeing right and he was; they were bright red clown shoes angled just so he could only see the tips peering from under the puzzle of walkways two stories under him.

"Ted…" There was no movement or reply. John's intuition was telling him to run; something was off, and this was all wrong, but he was frozen in curiosity. He knew Ted was up to another prank, but he couldn't remember if he had ever told the guys about his fear of clowns, but either way, he found himself yelling in anger and fear wanting a response, and he would get one.

"TED? GOSH DANG IT! QUIT HORSING AROUND. I'M TRYING TO GET THIS STUFF DONE OVER HERE!" John shouted down from his ladder, wanting to throw his crescent wrench down at Ted, or Garth, or whomever…whatever it was, but he didn't. He froze in terror when only half of it came into view to look up at John.

It moved slowly, but it finally moved, turning its head slowly to look up at him crookedly. It smiled waving all four fingers, as if it was waving to a child or an infant. Its smile caused John's skin to prickle with goosebumps. Its smile seemed to reach from ear to ear with so many teeth as sharp as a barracuda's and half as thick as tusks with red lipstick tracing its thin lips that matched its shoes. Its eyes were void of light and showed no emotion, no hint of life or death—hollowed black jewels that absorbed any light in the factory.

John's hair stood up as he stared into its lifeless, black eyes. It stared back smiling angrily—a smile that could make your blood run cold and your hair turn grey. The clown quit waving and quit smiling, but John could feel the anger still. The clown stood back upright and it was out of sight just like that, except the shoes, the shoes never moved…until John took a step down off the ladder and the clown took a step forward up the stairs.

YOU'RE IT

Steven was walking the streets he had always walked with only one difference: no one was around. The city seemed to have been abandoned overnight without a hint of what could've caused such a massive evacuation. Everything had been left behind in the middle of whatever anyone was doing. Food was on plates with only bites taken and there was an undeniable eerie feeling attached to Steven's spine. As he walked by a sports bar, the TV on the patio was still on and changing channels every minute. It was just enough time to let the viewer comprehend what he was seeing, and none of it was good. Every city shown was as abandoned and hollow as the ground he stood on. He didn't want to believe what he was seeing and decided to walk away, but his first step taken caused a reaction that made him jump.

The TV went black, but there was no one there to turn it off. The power didn't cut out, because some lights were still lit around the bar and most of the street lights as well, at least the ones that hadn't been bulldozed over. Steven looked around wildly hoping to see a glimpse of a brother, a friend, or even a stranger. He screamed at the top of his lungs. "HELLO! IS ANYBODY OUT THERE!? HELLLLOOO!!!"

His throat was starting to scratch at the base and become hoarse with every scream. A giggle came from down an alleyway across the street, and Steven instantly regretted not wanting to be alone. It was a giggle of pure evil and not earthly. When he finally turned to see, his eyes widened, the hair on his body stood straight up and he felt dread. A man was being dragged behind a corner while mouthing pleas and coughing up blood. The laughs continued around the corner of the wall as steady as the man was being dragged out of sight, but once the man was out of Steven's view, the laughing stopped and so did the dying man's coughing. Steven turned to run but was cut off by whatever it was. The little boy was around the age of seven with jet black hair and hollow eye sockets. His pale flesh seemed almost translucent with all the blue highways running up and down his limbs. Steven wanted to talk to him, wanted to get a word out, but he couldn't speak.

It was as if he had gone mute. When he finally mustered up enough courage, the little boy touched Steven lightly on the arm and ran off laughing and saying, "TAG! You're it."

NEWBORN

A father walked toward the nursery to console his crying baby in the middle of the night as he had done since the baby had come home with him, and only him. His wife never left the delivery bed, and Thomas really hadn't had time to mourn, but he had been pondering on her last words to him. "Don't bring it home." She had said it faintly, in a whisper, as her life's fluid leaked out in a much more rapid pace than they could put it back into her. It was a curious thing for a mother to say about her newborn, but the more Thomas dwelled on it, the more he remembered: the sounds of the crying, the wailing of the blood-covered baby and the way it had sounded, and the way it had stopped when its mother passed, as if relieved or calmed by the death of his mother.

Thomas was tired and still in a haze; his eyes were cloudy and with all the lights off in the house, it was hard to walk around but not impossible. This had been his home for some years, and he could navigate his way in the dark, but the baby's cries echoed making it seem as though his son could be anywhere. By the time Thomas reached the nursery, all cloudiness and doubt went away when he saw lying in the crib, wailing that high-pitch wail that only he and every neighborhood dog seemed to hear. When Thomas finally reached the crib to pick up his son, all cries and sobs grew louder, almost numbing Thomas and buckling him at the knees, but he held on to it, his son, while the other hand reached out, grabbing the crib and letting his knees hit the hardwood softer than they initially would have.

Thomas looked down to see how his son had fared the fall but nothing had changed. Cries and sobs continued; if anything, they were louder now. Thomas took his hand away from the rail of the crib to better hold his son, and that's when his son's neck draped over his hand like a piece of a garment made of flesh. Thomas screamed thinking he had just broken his son's neck during the fall, but when he looked again through tear-filled eyes, his son's face returned from behind its shoulders like an owl turning back to clean something off its back, but this was a human vertebrae incapable of such acts, but it was happening, whether the father believed it or not.

His son stared back at Thomas, blank-faced and emotionless with eyes a mixture of blood and black mud. Crickets had even stopped singing their song in unison and a wave of eerie silence surrounded the both of them. The child turned to look in the corner of the room angrily after the smallest of creeks echoed like someone had shifted their weight over the old wood floor of the house. When Thomas saw what his son was looking at, it wasn't anger that filled him but terror.

"I told you not to bring it home."

DANTE'S DESCENT

CHAPTER 1

They were walking for some time and in the same direction, with the only evidence being a trail of white hollowed-out footsteps in the snow following them, like an invisible stalker, up to where they were. The fog was disappearing and the cold wind that had gripped at their jackets and tugged at their warmth died down with every step towards the top. Dante smiled at Virginia reassuring it was not in vain, but his smile must have betrayed him because her fear never changed, but maybe it was just the cold. The cold had a wide range of effects on the human soul and made extreme capabilities of the simplest men come out in spades. The cold could reveal the subconscious it seemed, causing brave men to cower. Some cowards rose to the occasion while other cowards further burrowed themselves in despair and took another way down, or simply sat and let death come to them. There was something primal about being out there and fighting against Mother Nature's creatures and the elements she brought with her.

Dante had never been a religious man but that didn't stop him from forming his own thoughts or opinions on the matter, and hell, to him this was nothing like in the books. It was somewhere that was freezing, somewhere dark. Darker than any abyss, it was like walking through a wormhole, a void in space, but it was the cold that was punishment. Cold can be so cold it almost feels like your flesh is burning, but that's not the case, and so it is on earth. This mountain was a race against themselves, and these two were almost to the finish line, but along with fading footsteps, their memory also faded. There must have been more people, but only these two lovers were walking up into the clouds now. These were thoughts not to be had or even shared with the woman he planned on proposing to. This experience was meant to be unforgettable, but moments of the journey, maybe even everything up until now, was all forgotten.

They walked and walked with every fifty feet or so being a curtain of calmer weather, like being stuck in a car wash where the front is exiting clean and dry and the back is still being brushed and hosed down with flakes of snow. The conversations were few and far between, not for the loss of words, but for the fear of reality, fear of not truly knowing what the other was thinking and too scared to ask. All they had was the task at hand, and it was one that took focus, and not the left-foot, right-foot kind of focus, but the kind where you had to keep a gust of wind from grabbing you and sending you over the ledge because you had lost your footing. Dante honestly thought of all the ways to propose, and this seemed the most logical. They were both outdoorsy, they both camped in all elements, and they both were into world traveling and the extreme things that locals and tourists did, even if it meant death, but this was the closest to it they had ever come and before it would end, they might be formally introduced.

The top of the mountain was as calm and beautiful as the pearly gates. It does not only look but felt as if they had reached heaven itself. The sky was a warm orange with light purples streaming through, like silk translucent ribbons. The sun was like the presence of God. The warmth was so comforting, Dante felt as though he could fly away with the breeze to make the clouds his home. He didn't know how she felt, but he knew this was the moment that was to start the rest of their lives together. They walked over to ledge hand in hand and stared out into the beyond. Dante looked down and saw darkness; there was no mountainside, no clouds or snow. It was as if the sun was not allowed beneath where they stood, and instead of giving it anymore thought, he turned on one knee, giving her back to the dark void, and he took out the suede blue box from within his jacket to propose what he thought would be for the rest of their lives, but when he knelt, a river of rippling cracks gave way, sounding like a rib in a mastiff's mouth.

In the next second, his love, his reason for even coming out here, was falling down to the bottom along with snow and the broken ledge. Dante's hands reached out frantically grasping at air, stumbling on snow and ice as he ran to her aide, but his stumbling was the only thing to keep him from going over with her. It wasn't the look on her face or her bulging eyes but the sound of horror that came from her mouth; it was like that of a mother finding out her only child had passed away. The scream seemed to go on for the length of the fall, but Dante would never know because his own screams drowned out whatever echo of hers made it back up to the peak where he stood. His bare hands dug into the cold snow, as he kneeled over looking down screaming for his would-be bride, but all he heard in return was his own voice screaming back at him. After an hour of staring down into the darkness wishing, hoping for a hand to reach up from the black water that swallowed her like quicksand, he sat down with his head in his lap and his back to the mountain crying, sobbing like a child.

Once his crying subsided and the silence returned to the mountain, he looked up and noticed the sun hadn't moved the entire time; it was as if time stood still or the sky had been painted with no signs of brush marks. Dante stared, feeling unsettled. He had just watched the love of his life fall to her death, but Dante had felt unsettled even before they arrived at the top, and he knew she had felt the same. The look on her face said it all when he turned around, but he kept going and she followed. Now, she was dead and he had to make the trip back down alone...all alone. This sparked an assembly line of questions taking on different forms, but answers were like rabbits breeding more questions. Dante stood back up and walked to the ledge not wanting to believe his love was gone. He screamed for her once more but only heard silence. He strained his eyes to look further down, but snow, wind, and blackness engulfed the base of the mountain.

He turned to pick up his backpack and head back down, but he noticed hers was gone. The snow and wind had blown away whatever trace of footprints she had left; it was as if he had imagined everything, as if he had walked up here alone, but that wasn't right. He could still hear her screams in his head, and he was determined to find her at the bottom, dead or alive, but he never knew how he would find her if he did at all. The snow might bury her; wolves and other scavengers in the dark would make quick work of flesh and bone, and if she was alive, she was seriously injured or **wanting** to die. Dante had to get to her quickly. His love wouldn't end; even if she was dead, he would find her. He would travel through nine circles of hell for his dearest love, and the things he would do to get her back would make even Satan cringe. He swung his backpack onto his shoulder while he slid his other arm into the strap. Looking back down the trail he walked, where **they** walked, he took his first step, but when he did, the walkie-talkie in his inner jacket pocket went off and the voice matched his lover's.

"Dante! Dante, please. help me." The voice yelled in a whisper tone as if not wanting to be heard by anyone or anything else.

Dante scrambled trying to unzip his jacket and get to it, but thick gloves and heart-wrenching adrenaline turned all fingers into thumbs. Her pleas for help continued but were interrupted by something else.

CHAPTER 2

He had stopped hearing his lover's voice, and was interrupted by the walkie-talkie's frequency, like a high pitched bullet shot into his eardrum. Just like that, her end was cut off. The sound of her cries and sobs sent Dante into a whirlwind, not because she was in pain but because they were pleas for help, something was after her. Dante reached into his backpack and grabbed his hook for climbing, but he didn't intend to do any climbing; it was for protection from whatever might be down there with Virginia. Maybe it would decide to come up where he was, and if it did, he would be prepared this time and not fumbling at the zipper.

The backpack was still heavy with equipment, slowing him down. These decisions were time-consuming; so, he decided he would leave it all except for a few things he could carry on his person or in his hands. He searched through the bag with sounds of Virginia's pleas, begging for help, in the back of his mind, but it was always interrupted by that other sound, that un-human sound. He grabbed the rope and flung it over his head and one shoulder to strap around him. He also grabbed a compass, some foods, a flashlight, batteries and the walkie-talkie, a flask, and two climbing axes. Dante looked through the bag once more to make sure he had grabbed everything of importance and necessity and tossed the rest aside, shedding at least fifty pounds of gear.

He continued walking through curtains of weather as they had on the way up. The weather seemed to be getting colder and the fog was rolling in, teamed up with flakes of frost made it near impossible just to walk, so he reached for the mountainside to keep a gauge of safety and ledge. Dante walked and walked, stopping every so often to check in on the walkie-talkie, but there was never a reply, just silence, and he knew he couldn't keep checking in because it wasn't as if he had an endless supply of batteries. Dante had walked for at least five hours before finding a clue, a memory of what was before they had made it to the top. The lonely groom kneeled down in the snow to pick up a backpack but it wasn't his. He had left that back near the top, and it wasn't Virginia's. The color was wrong, but here, it was on the side of a mountain. He searched the grounds kicking snow and sweeping his feet from side to side like a metal detector, but there was nothing else, no sign of a camp or any clue as to anyone ever having been there.

The temperature dropped along with the sun, and the harder he walked to stay warm, the more he would sweat, frozen beads fell off his flesh, falling to the ground like a walking ice sculpture losing pieces of himself. Winds howled and memories returned as if he had lost his conscience piece by piece during the way up and was finding it on the way down. There had been more than just Dante and his bride-to-be; there had been a group of them. The number of climbers was still a bit hazy, but he knew for a fact there were more because he was staring at one of them in the distance. Even in the windy flurry, that bright traffic orange shown through like a wine stain on a white carpet.

The face was pale with a thin film of ice covering it, and sharp icicles had formed in his beard. The man seemed to be staring beyond Dante, like a scarecrow standing on its own in the middle of nowhere. Dante called out not knowing what to make of the situation, wondering how long he had been standing there, waiting. Time was of the essence and none could be wasted on some type of pranks or whatever this was, so he moved forward clutching both climbing axes in each hand ready for whatever might happen. When Dante finally reached the frozen roadblock, there was still no movement, not an inhale or an exhale, no shivering or reaction to the freezing cold. He noticed nothing that gave away this man was still alive, and then he blinked, trying to reveal a sinister smile as the frozen dead flesh chipped away from around his mouth, and Dante's blood got even colder.

Dante moved forward swinging up faster than the dead man could move, and the climbing axe caught him under the jaw, ripping through skin and bone, but there was no other sound, no scream or even a grunt. He had on the same smile he had been smiling before, but this time his eyes moved from Dante to the ledge. As if on command, a woman's voice screamed in horror and echoed throughout the mountain tops. He yanked the climbing axe free and shoved the frozen man against the hard cold mountain, causing a short flurry of snow to rain down on the both of them.

Before Dante could ask just one of his many questions, the frozen man pushed back and he was strong. He kept pushing, never letting off, and heading in the same direction as the ledge. The ledge was now several more steps away before Dante would fall, and his bride to be was counting on him. He had to save Virginia, and instead of fighting back, he used the dead man's momentum against him and with lightning quick speed, he cut a hand free from his jacket, grabbing the other hand and turning to throw the dead man over his shoulder and slamming him to the ground. The frozen man's face never changed; it stared and smiled the entire time.

"Let's see how funny this is." With both climbing axes wrapped around the dead man's neck, Dante pulled apart his axes along with the man's head from his shoulders. Sounds of bone and ice seemed to sound the same up here, but there was no other sound — no screams or grunts, no pleas or accusations, just staring eyes and the same smile that seemed to know what was to happen on this mountain and far worse, what was happening to his love. When Dante kicked the man's head off the ledge, the body stood up and ran off the ledge following the head, but it turned in mid-air to wave bye with the one hand he did have, mocking Dante, while the other hand moved like a spider for the ledge and down the mountainside. Dante not only felt but knew he was in hell.

CHAPTER 3

Dante gathered whatever sanity he had left and took off, running as if he were trying to beat gravity and the dead man's fall to the bottom. Eventually, Dante stopped, realizing there was nothing. no surrounding mountains, no cold to pierce his flesh and touch the bones. There was just him and the ground he was standing on, and even then, with every step, he should've heard a thud or crunching sound of the gathered snow under his boot, but again nothing. If this was a sign of something to come, he wouldn't wait around for it, so he ran to it. Not only was he surrounded by nothingness, but he felt as though maybe that's what he was running towards as well, caught in some maze with no entrance or exit. He stopped once more, remembering the way the headless man waved while falling and the way his hand had followed like a giant tarantula.

He took steps towards the ledge to look over, and he saw darkness. There was no base camp or aircraft, just darkness. Suddenly, something grabbed him by the ankle and yanked, making him lose his footing. He slipped, hitting the ground only to gain momentum and slide off the side. He turned, swinging both climbing axes wildly trying to have one catch but there was no such luck. Dante didn't know how much longer he had before he hit the ground, so with all his concentration and power, he swung one last time to catch and imbed between the crevice of two rocks. The weight and momentum of the fall ripped the axe from its place; after another couple feet of falling, he fell on his feet. It was a one in a million landing, or maybe he had help from something he couldn't see. He walked towards another ledge, but he was at the bottom of a dark plateau of white carpet with mounds scattered throughout his vision from left to right. He went to the closest one, revealing a face of a stranger but a face he knew. There were another mound and another stranger reminiscent of some time ago.

When there were two mounds left, realization hit Dante of the next two faces he would see, but he had to see for himself, and he did. If it wasn't her flesh he could save anymore, it would have to be her soul.

LORD OF THE DEAD FLIES

Bonus Story

DAY 1: MORNING

A car drove through a small town on the outskirts of a bigger town with more amenities. The social worker drove and still tried to talk to the kids, even when she was about to drop them off and not a single word had been spoken during the entire trip. "I know you guys don't wanna talk, but I'm going to give you my number, and we can talk about whatever you want, whenever you want. If you'd rather talk to someone else, Luke, my husband Fernando is a good listener, and he's into all that outdoors stuff." The car was empty of voices, but the radio could be heard. When they came to a red light, she slipped Luke her card and looked in the back to the little girl, who was grim-faced and sad, and said, "Anything." Then she looked to Luke. "Anytime. I hope you guys know that."

The light turned green and the vehicle was in motion once more to their final destination, which was the kids' next home, even when it may be temporary. The town was so small there wasn't room for any buildings except for those necessary for life: a single bank, a grocery store, the police station, and the smallest of hospitals. Their new temporary home was now in sight, almost resembling a farmhouse, but the iron gates that surrounded the premises made it look like a prison and gave off the feeling of an insane asylum. The driveway was as long as a football field, and that was just to the entrance of the gate. There was at least another three hundred yards to the front door. The estate was mostly clear cut with no shrubbery except for three trees, two of which were close enough for a hammock to be placed; the other was by the fence to help anyone get from one side to the other. There was also a guest house that offers an exit through the back iron gate and into the forest.

Kids were playing Frisbee in the front yard, the two caretakers were standing outside talking with each other, smoking cigarettes and staring at their cell phones, while the third caretaker watched everything. As the car pulled into the security protected gate, Luke noticed two kids in the tree behind the two careless caretakers, and with a couple of climbed branches, they disappeared into the forest.

"Where we going?" Timothy asked.

Maurice kept walking, knowing if he told Timothy the truth, he would want to turn back around. "Just a little further, you'll see." Maurice walked through some branches like a curtain revealing the big secret showing Timothy where he'd been going to smoke and relax without being watched. "It's abandoned. Must've been part of the orphanage before it was an orphanage."

"What are we doing here?" asked Timothy, showing his age through his tone.

Maurice reached into his pocket and took out a pack of cigarettes with a lighter. The pack was old and basically had lost its shape, but there were two cigarettes left in perfect condition.

"We shouldn't be here. What if someone saw us leave?" Timothy asked, nervously.

"Trust me, no one saw us leave. Would you fucking relax? You're making me nervous," Maurice said, starting to get irritated with one of the younger kids, or what all the older kids called desirables.

"Ok fine, but as soon as you're done, we're going back," said Timothy.

"Yea, yea, soon as I'm done," Maurice said in a dismissive manner. As he put his head down to let the cigarette meet the lighter, Timothy caught a glimpse of a body in the window staring down at them. He was startled and shoved Maurice to turn around and witness what he had just seen, but the fear and adrenaline were too much for Maurice, knocking him down to the ground.

"Someone's in the house," Timothy said while pointing at the window to show Maurice, but nothing was there to stare back.

"GOD, DAMNIT! What the fuck is your problem? I knew I should've come alone instead of trying to do something nice. Just be lucky I have another one," Maurice said.

"I swear; I saw someone staring at us."

"Who gives a shit. Let him stare. Maybe he's a bum who wants a cigarette, but now, he's not getting one."

Timothy knew something was wrong with the man and he wanted something but it wasn't a cigarette. "I just wanna go back home."

"That shit hole is no home, and those caretakers aren't your parents. They come and leave at 5 o'clock. If you wanna go 'home' so bad, just go. This is my last one and I plan on smoking it." Maurice threw the pack away and repeated the same steps as before to light his last cigarette, bending down to light it. This time, the man in the window was behind Maurice and staring at Timothy with rage-filled eyes. Timothy fell to the ground, crawling backward in panic, trying to gain his footing but slipping with every step taken.

"Dude, what the fuck is your deal?" Maurice asked, starting to sound a little nervous himself seeing the horror in Timothy's eyes. When he turned, his horror matched Timothy's. The man staring was foaming blood out of his mouth, while making growling sounds from the depth of his stomach. Like a cobra striking a field mouse, the zombie tackled Maurice to the ground and viciously started to bite wherever it could as many times as it could. "HELP ME, PLEASE!" Maurice screamed a blood-curdling scream, but the zombie never stopped or let up.

Timothy reached for Maurice's arm, trying to pull him away from the zombie's grip, but the man bit at Timothy and broke the skin. Timothy fell down now for the third time but when he got back up, he didn't wait around any longer to risk falling again and headed back to the orphanage. As he ran deeper and deeper into the forest, the screams eventually stopped, and Timothy knew what that meant. The boy reached the orphanage and covered the bite with his long sleeve, so he wouldn't have to explain where he was or what had happened. He snuck right back into the groove of things and noticed a car at the front entrance with two kids and a social worker walking up to the front door. As they walked through the grounds and up to the door, the kids stopped doing whatever it was they were doing and watched the newcomers, while the two caretakers were oblivious to the whole thing. The girl, April, was holding onto her brother's hand and holding her stuffed animal in front of her face as to hide from the watching eyes.

"It's ok, Li'l Foot. We only have to stay here for a little while," said Luke to his little sister.

She looked up from behind her stuffed monkey and looked around the grounds to see what kind of home they would be living in, but instead, she focused on the distraught kid who looked ill and terrified.

"Promise?" she asked.

"Promise," Luke replied.

They continued to walk past the crowd of kids and went into the custody of the only caretaker who was actually watching: Ms. Clark.

"Hi, Ms. Clark. Here is Luke and his little sister, April," said Mrs. Rodrigues.

"Hi Luke, hi April. I'm Ms. Clark, and I'm the resident caretaker or principal, if you will. I understand you won't be here very long, but that doesn't mean we can't get to know one another." She looked at Ms. Rodrigues when the kids never answered or replied and finished the conversation with her. "I can take it from here, thank you."

They both turned to Mrs. Rodrigues and each took turns giving hugs and saying their goodbyes. "Remember, if you need anything, I'm a phone call away." She looked to Ms. Clark, nodded and headed back down the long driveway to her car.

"Well, I'm sure you two want to get settled in and cleaned up after such a journey. You'll have plenty of time to meet everyone afterwards."

"Thank you, Ms. Clark, but we shouldn't be here too long," Luke said wanting to make sure she remembered the court's ruling.

"That's right, total slip of the mind. When kids come here, it's usually for a while. Either way, I'm sure April would like to make some new friends," said Ms. Clark looking at April, but she saw nothing but a stuffed animal. All the while, April stared at the pale boy. "Hmm, okay, well follow me."

They continued walking up the steps. April looked up from her stuffed animal to see the enormous old colonial style house that seemed haunted to the very core, but when they walked through the doors, it was like night and day. The inside was clean and all remodeled to look nothing like the skin of the home. They walked up what had to be the longest staircase they had ever seen, and every story was like a crosswalk of rooms and more stairs. Ms. Clark seemed to be leading them to the very top but stopped a story short. At the end of the hallway was their bedroom. Ms. Clark opened the door to let the siblings in to get adjusted while she stood at the door and watched their faces. She always wanted to get a read on the children when they first realized this was home. Yet again, she was disappointed but always hopeful. "Please children, if there is anything I can do to make you feel more at home, please let me know," Ms. Clark said while winking at April. April never returned the gesture or even smiled, so Ms. Clark figured it would be best to leave them be for now. "I'll have one of the boys come get you children later for breakfast. See you then."

She turned and walked away leaving the siblings to unpack and settle in, but neither one moved for the luggage; they both sat on each bed facing one another.

"Remember, just till my birthday and then we can get our own place," Luke said winking at April as Ms. Clark had done.

"Promise?" asked April, laughing nervously.

"Cross my heart and hope to die."

DAY 1: MIDNIGHT

The children heard knocks downstairs, but no one moved to the door. The day's events and what had happened to the others was enough to never move again. The little ones huddled close to one another while the elders, like Jack and Luke, stood on each side of the door waiting to pounce on whatever might walk through, but seconds turned into a couple of minutes and all they could hear was the sound of their own breath. When Jack turned to sit back down with his raggedy band of misfits, there was a knock at the door, their door this time. No one moved to open it except one of the little boys who knew it was the soldier he had seen on the roof top from the window. When he opened it, a man stood in the doorway dressed all in black and tactical gear from head to toe with shades of different reds covering his flesh.

The man searched the room from left to right. Before he spoke, a loud scream echoed throughout the hallway and room. The children all huddled as close as their bodies would allow, like bending a jigsaw piece to fit somewhere it didn't. The man had looked to his left to find the source of the scream already on him and too late to get a true shot; it was as if the zed knew to creep up on him but couldn't contain the rage when in the perimeter to strike. He raised his arm to shoot, and the bullet missed, but the caretaker didn't, taking full advantage of the marksman's misfortune, biting down on exposed flesh, like a dog with a bone, shaking her head violently. He dropped the gun down to his free hand and with the butt of the gun, he beat down on her head only to strengthen her bite on his forearm, so he took action and the next move was a bullet through the temple.

He stood in the hallway holding his arm. The children now felt safe knowing there wasn't anyone left in the house and they moved towards their savior only to be rejected like so many other times in life. "STOP! Do not move any closer. I've been bitten and will turn into whatever that lady was. You kids need to get out of here, now!"

The one who had opened the door looked at the soldier, and with all sincerity, asked, "Where do we go?"

The soldier looked around the room and saw his dead comrades staring back at him, but after a couple of blinks, the children's faces returned but the eyes were the same. Fear, anger, sadness, but the one the soldier saw unanimously was a disappointment. "Look, you have two options. If you stay here, you need to destroy that staircase. Get everything you need, like water, batteries, and food. If you destroy the staircase, they can't come up. My bodysuit has a GPS attached and some people will come for this." He pulled out both vials of blood to show the children. "I don't trust these people, and I don't think you should either. That's why I say you go with option two." As he handed both vials to Luke, he said, "Leave here and head to the mountains. There is a camp up there with park rangers, and you can stay there and give them the vials. Just tell Mr. Rodrigues that Wyatt couldn't make it." He turned to walk away leaving the weapons behind, taking only one sidearm.

"Where are you going?" asked one of the little boys.

The soldier looked around the room at all the scared children and said, "Don't follow me. Remember what I've told you, and you'll be okay."

The soldier disappeared, leaving only a trace of echoing steps on wood that eventually came to a stop after the main door closed. All the kids looked to one another as if Christmas had come and gone, knowing they were back to square one and all alone once more. All the young children looked to Luke for answers, and Jack could tell he was losing influence, if he ever had any. Maybe it wasn't influenced but fear he used to control the younger ones, but now the world was upside down, and there were worse things to fear.

Before one of the young ones could speak and give the floor to Luke, Jack interrupted abruptly and not sounding like his usual self.

"We have to get out of here; we have guns and a head start," Jack said.

Luke knew it was an idea but not a great one, and he didn't want to further impose on the alpha of the group, but he didn't want to get his little sister or himself killed either. The logic was sound, but there were too many factors involved, too many kids to corral in the same direction, and too much noise. They would stick out running in a small herd. "I agree, but it's too dangerous for all of us to leave together. We need to leave in small groups an hour apart from each other."

Jack looked wearily at Luke, knowing he was up to something. He knew he wanted to get rid of him so he could rule over the little twerps. "What are you up to, Luke? Why wouldn't we just leave together?"

Luke was getting irritated at the situation, but mostly with Jack. In a time like this, he could still be so ignorant and self-involved with losing his place in this small society, but it was his place and when you had only that one, you would fight for it, maybe even kill for it. "Fine Jack, then I'll go first," He looked around the room as the soldier did and saw what he had seen: nothing but frightened little children, and each one was in danger. "Who wants to come with April and me?"

Almost every single child moved except for the couple of lackeys who would not leave Jack's side no matter how hard he beat them, and when Jack had seen that he would be left alone with mostly children, which wasn't enough. That would never be enough for Jack. "So, you can leave us here to die? I don't think so, Luke," Jack said with such confirmation, it was as if he already had a gun pointed at him.

"Camp Ivy isn't that far from here..." Said Ralph nervously, feeling the tension in the air once more.

"How far is it?" Luke asked, ignoring Jack.

This time it was one of the youngins named Rob who answered and answered while walking over to their group. "Two miles. But we can take the trail Maurice used to take to smoke back by the abandoned home. He always brought me to keep watch..."

Luke not wanting to be mean, cut him off as politely as possible knowing a child could babble on such as his little sister and jump from topic to topic. "Thank you Rob. We have a destination and a distance. So we have April, me, Simon, Maddie, and Ralph..."

Jack interrupted "You mean Piggy." Giggling to him and his band of misfits

"And me." Said Rob, looking back at Jack while standing next to Luke.

Jack Noticed he was down one and steadily losing influence even after receiving seniority once Maurice died; now, Luke Is here and older by a year. Jack stood silently while taking stock at those on his side of the room. Roger of course was there, Jack's best friend and most loyal, the twins Sam and Eric would go wherever the other was, so there was no real loyalty there, and lastly there was Will, who was the same age as Rob. A child that could offer no real help to Jack except as a body. "I think we should stay.

Now Luke was really getting irritated because Jack's vanity and pride were going to get them all killed, but he would have to play politics in order to get not only himself out of this but his baby sister, the last living family member he had, the only true friend who had been through almost everything he had. He would fight for her, and if it came down to it, he would kill for her. "It was your idea to leave, now you want to stay, fine Jack, then we all stay here, but we have to be on the same page. We need to break down those stairs. We have enough people here to do everything we need to, but we have to do it **now.**"

Jack could see the irritation and anger flash red on Luke's face, and it was almost amusing to Jack. He might even respect him if it were only the two of them, but there were eyes watching and his pride was on the line. "So, go ahead. Do what you gotta do, and I'll do what I gotta do." He walked over to the bag and grabbed two pistols with no ammunition, showing his true ignorance, he never checked to see if the pistols he picked even had ammunition, and Luke struggled on whether to tell him or not.

"Fine. Okay, besides April and I, who else has used a gun or rifle before?" Luke said looking around the room at the children. They were scared children who had never held a parent let alone a pistol, but one raised his hand and stepped forward. Luke walked over to the bag and grabbed three pistols and one of the rifles emptying the bag. He distributed them to his little sister and the boy named Simon; he kept one pistol for himself and the rifle as well.

"Who said you could take all those?" Jack demanded.

"Whoever knows how to use one needs to have one. We can't protect the house or each other if one of you doesn't know how to use one, and not to mention **you** grabbing two. Now, we have to take care of those steps." Luke was almost starting to plead and Jack knew it. Luke could see he was about to make him beg or degrade himself in order to get what he wanted, but before he could, Simon spoke up.

"I'll take the back stairs."

Ralph nodded. "I'll go with Simon. I'll go grab some tools but I'll need some help."

April looked up to her big brother. "I'll go with them to help stand look out," she said.

Luke looked down at his baby sister, his only family left, and nodded in agreement. "Jack, Roger, I'll go with you guys to help with the front steps."

Jack interrupted Luke, not taking the consideration lightly. "You, Roger, and Eric can go. Someone has to babysit these little shits, and it probably should be the oldest, which would be me." Before he took his seat, he walked over to Roger and handed him the second pistol showing trust but not without reason.

Luke expected nothing less, but since April would not be under his watch, he didn't mind at all, as long as he didn't have to spend another minute with him. "Fine, let's make this quick," Luke said, not really wanting to be in Roger or Eric's presence either.

The night was starting to fade away into the dawn while the last step was being pulled up. Luke looked to April and smiled knowing they had won a small victory until there were sounds of glass shattering and multiple bangs at the door, erratic knocks with no purpose of wanting to borrow sugar.

DAY 1: BREAKFAST

There was a knock on their door, and a voice behind it shouted, "BREAKFAST'S READY!" followed by steps running down the hall, away from their door and down the steps.

"You ready, April?" Luke asked, and she nodded in agreement and stood up to reach for her brother's hand. When they reached downstairs, there were multiple tables and only three were occupied, but even then, seats were available. It was as if there were three separate gangs, while one table sat the adults but only the groundskeeper sat there. As each of them looked around the room, there was a boy of mid height who looked even shorter because of how big he was sideways. He started to walk over to them with an accepting grin and his hand out for Luke to shake. "Hey, I'm Ralph, nice to meet you."

Luke shook his hand and replied with the usual formalities that his parents usually committed. "I'm Luke, and this is my sister April."

"Hi, April. Well, you guys should go ahead and fix your plates. That table there is where I sit if you guys want to join us. The other table is where the undesirables sit. Jack is the guy staring at you, and they're missing two orphans. Maurice probably ran away again, and Tim is in the nurse's office."

Luke could feel Jack's eyes on him, but he was too busy looking at the groundskeeper sitting alone at the adult table. "Where's Ms. Clark?" Luke asked Ralph.

"Oh, she is actually taking care of Tim. She used to be a nurse. He just started throwing up and then passed out. She sent me to you before she took him into her office."

All the kids were staring at Luke and his sister and not one of them looked happy to have more roommates or 'competition.'

"What happened to him?" Luke asked while fixing April's plate and being very aware of all the eyes on them.

"He was bitten by something, but he wouldn't say what did it. The security guard Hank is out looking for it."

"I hope he finds it," Luke replied.

"Me too. Well, I'll let you guys get to it. Just sit wherever makes you most comfortable," Ralph said before turning to walk away back to his table. Luke poured his little sister a small cup of juice, and made her a plate with all the syrup she wanted. He headed to a table that would be their own with no one else but even if they didn't sit with them, they could still hear them. As Luke and his sister April sat down the groundskeeper stood up and went back to his daily duties, and before Luke even got the chance to take his first bite, Jack interrupted with a query taking advantage of an all kid room.

"You too good to sit with us?" Jack asked in a bully tone.

"No, not at all. It's just been a long day and we didn't feel like talking much."

"Sounded like you had a lot to say to Piggy over there," Jack snapped back instantly.

"Ralph was being polite..."

"So, he can talk, just not with the likes of us," Jack interrupted looking for confirmation amongst the ones he sat with.

"That's not what I was going to say," Luke replied getting irritated at the accusations.

"What you meant was to disrespect me and my friends. What you meant..."

Now it was Luke who did the interrupting, "If you would shut up and let me talk, you would know what I meant."

All the kids looked to Jack to see what he would do. The room was silent as a cemetery, and before Jack could respond, Ms. Clark entered the room. She was covered in blood and shaking from what she had witnessed, with her left hand holding the back of her right arm. The kids gasped not knowing what to make of it and Gary the groundskeeper ran back in the room to her side for consoling.

"It looks like Timothy will be going to the emergency room. Ms. Garcia and Ms. Smith will be taking him and will return shortly. Hank is still out looking for Maurice."

"Is he okay?" Eric asked and Sam right after, "What's wrong with him?"

"I honestly don't know...but for now, just eat your breakfast and I'll be back as soon as I'm cleaned up," Ms. Clark said in a tone that suggested she was ready for the day to be over.

"Why did both caretakers take him?" Luke asked not being able to wait till later.

She looked at Luke as if he had overstepped, but she answered all the same. "When Tim woke up he was not himself and bit Ms. Smith, it was a pretty bad bite and is going to need stitches, so Ms. Garcia had to drive for the both of them. Again... they should be back shortly." She turned to walk away even faster to avoid any more questions, and the groundskeeper followed.

Once she was gone, April turned to her brother and said, "I'm scared. I don't want to stay here anymore."

"It's ok, Li'l Foot. I'll protect you. Eat up and we'll hang out in our room and play Go Fish," Luke said to April as reassuring and convincing as he could.

Jack, irritated with the newcomer and threatened by his newbie status, again tried to belittle him in front of his little lackeys. "Who do you think you are asking all those questions?" he said, in the usual tough-guy tone.

Luke calmly retorted while looking directly into Jack's eyes, making it known he was not intimidated. "Just someone who would like to know the truth, so I can assess the situation. You see someone covered in blood from a single bite and you don't have any questions?"

Jack instantly regretted his position, and without thought, he spat out, "That's not what I meant."

Luke retorted once again. "Funny how that works," and the room went silent once more, but this time Jack stood up so quickly, his chair ricocheted off the back off his knees and slid back a couple feet. Luke looked at his baby sister and said, "Go to our room, April. Lock the door. Don't answer till I knock." Without debate or argument, she did as her brother asked and did it quickly, grabbing her plate and racing for the door, hidden behind her stuffed monkey as Jack's laughs echoed behind her.

"Hahaha. What's the matter? Don't want your girlfriend watching me kick your ass?" Jack said while laughing and snickering.

This time it was Luke who stood up, but before another move was made, they heard a door slam. Jack sat back down and so did Luke. Hurried footsteps scattered throughout the hall, and they were met with another pair of hurried footsteps. Ms. Clark's voice was the next thing they heard but in a panicked tone, "Did you find anything?"

Hank stared back with eyes of a lost child, and if anyone knew that look, it was Ms. Clark, but to see it in a grown man put her fears further into a spiral. "We need to barricade the windows. Lock the doors and barricade them too. Get everyone upstairs once we've finished, and....what happened to you?" Hank asked once he noticed, being too preoccupied with searching for the utility closet.

Ms. Clark clinched her shirt in fear because she didn't know what to be scared about. "Timothy is very sick. What's going on? You're frightening me. You look pale."

Hank finally found the closet, swinging the door open, he started to reply once the essentials hit the floor in a pile ready to be handed out. "Listen when I tell you to barricade the windows and lock the doors. We need everyone to help."

This time it was Jack who stood up to try and alpha the situation. "Everything okay, Ms. Clark?"

Ms. Clark was pissed that they were listening in on what was being said, and she couldn't control her temper any longer. "This conversation is for adults. When I need your help, I WILL ASK FOR IT!"

Jack looked to Luke to see if he was being laughed at, but it was his own lackeys who were doing the laughing, and another piece of Jack's control was slipping away, so he decided it was time for action because words weren't his specialty. Jack grabbed the nearest boy Rob, slapping him clean across the face, which made every boy at his table clinch in pain, almost feeling the hit themselves. "Never laugh at me again, you understand?" He said to no one in particular while scanning from left to right looking for a displeased face.

Luke stood up silently and walked over to Jack's table, not knowing what he would say yet or even why he did it. Maybe he was trying to break the tension or maybe just trying to find out intel for his own selfish reasons, but either way, he was already noticed by the entire table and couldn't turn back now. "You mind if I sit down?" Luke asked while looking Jack in the eye. Jack nodded in approval and Luke took the seat and leaned in so the adults could not listen in on their conversation. "Something isn't right. When April and I were coming in, I saw the Timothy boy coming back from the forest behind here holding his arm. I've heard another kid is missing..."

Jack, wanting to take control of the situation, started his own line of questioning. "Why are we even talking about this? Who do you think you are?"

Luke sat looking at Jack while measuring the next words he would use, knowing Jack was the sensitive type and had to be in control of anything or anyone. "Someone who has a little sister to look after, and people seem to be getting sick or disappearing, and I don't want either of those to happen to April or me." Everyone at the table and also the surrounding tables were listening in, and before

Luke could continue, the footsteps came back and eventually Hank came around the corner with Ms. Clark on his tail.

Ms. Clark spoke, not wanting Hank's fear to spread to the children. "Please don't be frightened, children; everything is going to be okay."

Hank interrupted, "They need to be told the truth. It was a man who bit Timothy and he nearly bit me. I also found Maurice on the way back, and whatever Timothy has, Maurice definitely has it too.

Ms. Clark was the one who interrupted this time. "What?! Where is he now?"

Hank replied almost seeming to get calmer the more he revealed his secret. "He's still out there. I shot him in the knee and it slowed him down, but he kept coming."

Sam and Eric both exhaled. "Woah!"

Luke asked another question, putting two and two together. "Timothy bit the nurse, so we have to assume they are both infected, and they have probably infected everyone in the hospital." Jack instantly felt stupid for not thinking the same thing.

Ms. Clark answered with a question. "Should we call the hospital or at least try and call Ms. Garcia?"

"Call Ms. Garcia first, and I'll instruct the boys on what to do," Hank replied.

Ms. Clark moved immediately into the other room to call from her cell phone while Hank walked over to the closest table but spoke loud enough for all the orphans to hear. "Sam and Eric, I need you two to stay by the front door, and do not let anyone in, no matter what. If you see someone who's infected, scream for me right away. Boys and girls nine and younger, go to your rooms and lock the doors. The rest of you, follow me." Everyone got up and followed the orders according to their age group and the ones that were old enough followed Hank outside the Dining Hall into the main entrance where the utility closet was.

"You two, Jack and the new kid, grab the hammers and start nailing boards on the windows, starting by the front door. The rest of you grab all the wood you can and place them on the floors in front of the windows."

As everyone dispersed to do their part, a window smashed in and Hank saw Maurice standing there with blood-shot eyes and a snapping jaw, screaming to enter with growls of hunger. And behind Maurice, stood the man from the woods.

DAY 2: DAWN

The last stair was being pulled up and one of the children screamed out, "They're coming!" Bangs at the forgotten unlocked door gave way to a mob of zombies lead by there once savior. They all searched wildly running throughout the first floor like a wild stampede with no direction in mind, just driven by hunger. The air carried pheromones of fear and stenches of released bladders. The kids could smell themselves in the air, and so could the dead. One looked up and screamed wildly, jumping for the missing staircase and crashing down to the basement. One after another like sheep following the other to their fall almost creating a ladder of bodies that Luke knew they would eventually climb.

Jack screamed out in a panic, "They're gonna get up here!"

Luke snapped back in a whispered lashing. "Shut up! Now they for sure know were up here." As the screams grew louder, the wails brought more zombies from outside all running for one purpose. "We need to get out of here. Is there any other way out?" Luke asked looking at the long-time residents.

The fat boy Ralph that everyone called Piggy spoke up. "There's the string that pulls the stairs down."

There were destruction and blood everywhere. Sounds of the hungry dead and clashing of windows breaking and wood splintering from the barricades on the window made it hard to focus. "Jack, go grab that string and take the kids upstairs. I'll keep them busy."

"How are you gonna keep them busy?" Jack asked, delaying their safety.

"You're wasting time. JUST GO!" A thud hit the floor and everyone screamed seeing the hand that reached the second-story floor. Jack immediately turned, running for the attic stairs with all the little ducklings on his tail. Luke ran over to the hands that were pulling themselves up until they made eye contact. It was the soldier who once helped them and gave them hope, but now he was someone or something wanting to take it all away. Luke grabbed the rifle and butted it against his head three times, eventually cracking his skull and sending him down to the first story floor. From his position, Luke could see out the front door and out into the lawn, he noticed one zombie faster than all the others, passing them as if they weren't even running, and he saw his eyes were on his own. The zombie reached the door and in some Olympian fashion, leaped for the second floor. The wooden rails caught him, hitting him in the chest. Luke took aim and with one clear shot, and the zombie dropped as quickly as he arrived.

Luke looked to his left and noticed most of the children were entering the attic, but the ladder of bodies was growing, and now some seemed to be able to jump high enough without any assistance or support. Luke ran for the stairs but was stopped, taken off balance from a hard tackle that knocked him to the ground. The next thing he heard was a gunshot, a life-saving bullet that dropped 167 lbs of dead weight onto him. He looked up to see his baby sister pushing the twice dead man's body aside and helping him to his feet. Luke now aware of what was happening pushed his sister ahead of him to run towards the staircase. The zombies on the first floor had now reached the second with ease, like a never-ending flood, and the blood filled bodies would eventually take the house away, or the children inside at least. The attic was dark and full of wide white eyes all looking at Luke except Jack and his lackeys.

"We need a plan; we can't stay up here forever," Luke said while in the background, the noise of bodies jumping up and down on the wood floor, arms extended reaching for the unseen children.

"What do you mean get out of here? This is the plan," Jack said back in his usual rebellious tone.

"What do we do for food? What do we do for ammo?" Luke said back but in his whispered yell.

"We cross that bridge when we come to it, but until then, we stay here."

"Fine, you can stay here and be in charge, April and I and whoever else wants to come can, and we'll leave for supplies."

"We have supplies downstairs," Simon spoke up from the darkness, watching everyone as he always did, an outsider with no reason to be. "But that'll only last so long. We can't stay in the attic forever."

Ralph stood up and walked behind Luke and April, as did most of the children.

"Isn't this cute. All the shits I've never gotten along with side with the new guy. That's fine; you guys can stay here, but once you leave, you can't come back, AND I get one of the vials of blood," Jack said as if he had them backed into a corner.

"Deal," Luke said reaching out his hand for Jack's but Jack turned and walked away to his group while Luke turned to his but not before tapping Jack on the back with a vial of blood. "We have to wait it out here until the zombies downstairs forget were up here. Get some sleep; I'll take first watch," he said while setting up a spot to sit and watch his new group of friends and liabilities. Everyone drained of everything except their soul fell asleep, deep asleep as the floor beneath them rumbled from stampeding feet and jumping zombies. mid-day had come and the rumbles were nonexistent with only one zombie left jumping, mindless as if it was born jumping. Luke moved April aside softly as to not wake her or anyone else and crept towards the window to get a look at the grounds, and they were empty.

There was an opening for them to leave, but they had to decide where to go from here. They had to get past whatever was left of the herd that had once inhabited the house. They had to move as a single unit and mind from now on or they would come to regret it. Luke turned back to his little sister and the other kids. They all seemed to be on the same clock because they were all waking up simultaneously. The others were waking up as well, all of them except Jack, and no one moved to wake him. Luke whispered to all the waking children on his side of the room. "Is there a way down without taking those attic stairs?"

Ralph answered with a solution. "We can take the snack elevator to the kitchen and out into the back yard," he said with cheerfulness, having a solution and peers actually listening to that solution.

"Great idea," Jack said sitting up. "So, one by one, that shouldn't take too long or get anyone killed."

"Do you have a better idea? This is because right now, that seems the best way out, quiet and safely. We don't need to shoot our way out and possibly bring more of those things back."

Jack smiled and Luke didn't like the smirk one bit. It was as if Luke had given him an idea, but there were already enough problems as is. "Well, you guys go ahead and get yourselves killed. We will be up here, safe and sound."

They all walked over to the small elevator shoot and surrounded it as if it was a holy site. "Ms. Clark would give me healthy snacks to help me lose weight...and sometimes I would use it to sneak in the kitchen."

"Fatty," Jack interrupted,

"Don't listen to him. Do you think you could fit more than one in there?" Luke said in a calming tone.

"No more than two at a time," Simon said, wiping the wall clean and showing the hazard sticker with weight restrictions.

"Is there somewhere to hide until everyone has made it to the kitchen?"

"The pantry," said a tiny voice, a little girl named Maddie. "It's huge in there."

"We have a plan now, so it's time to execute. We need a big kid to go with a little, and I'll go last since I weigh the most." No one moved to the elevator shoot, nervous at what would be at the bottom, but then the little girl named Maddie stepped forward so Simon stepped forward, being the second youngest to Luke in this group. They stepped in, closed the door, and went on down to the kitchen with no sounds given. Once the elevator stopped, there was a long pause of anxiousness waiting to see the elevator come back to the attic. After what seemed an eternity, the small cubby hole elevator arrived, and Ralph along with April entered.

As they entered before pressing the button Luke and April hugged and kissed one another on the cheek, Luke pressed the button to descend his little sister to the kitchen while in the background he could hear Jack and his little lackeys whispering followed by laughing and snickering as if they were about to be the butt of some joke. From what Luke could tell, Ralph and his little sister were about halfway down when he heard shots being fired from behind him. One missed but the other hit him in the shoulder and Luke using the momentum to avoid being hit again leaned forward to fall down on top of the elevator causing the cable pully to snap and free fall to the kitchen floor. Luke now knew what Jack was smiling about.

DAY 1: BRUNCH

Sam and Eric screamed at the sight of the dead intruders and ran off to hide while the others hurried towards the scene of the sounds. Hank yelled orders at the present children. "GET INTO THE OFFICE NOW!" He walked over to Jack and grabbed him by his shirt to also grab his attention "You are going to open the door and let them in on my command." He let go of Jack only for him to run into the office behind the others. "GARY!!!" Screamed Hank hoping he didn't disappear to the guest house or shed as others so lovingly called it. When no one answered or replied he realized Luke had been standing there the entire time waiting to help, waiting for a direction to go and be unleashed. He walked back into the utility closet where almost everything was kept except groceries and came out with two aluminum baseball bats. He handed one to Luke and talked to him instead of demanding in a calm tone and manner as if he was up to bat and getting a pep talk before walking to the plate.

"You are going to let them in and hide behind the door. Don't move or help until I've called for it." He walked back a couple feet and placed the bat against the wall only to walk back to Luke and take out his pistol. "If these shots don't take them down the bat is plan B," he said while counting the ammo in the magazine. Luke walked over into position with his hand on the knob while looking at Hank awaiting the order. A nod of confirmation and Luke twisted his wrist, turning the knob and whipped opened the door so fast and hard if it wasn't for his feet he would've smacked himself with it.

They did as Hank predicted but he didn't predict a 3rd zombie. Shots fired one after another, one chipped away at the door making Luke slam it shut in an involuntary spasm and grabbing the attention of the last zed to enter. Hank after finishing off the magazine pulled the trigger a couple more times in hopes for another round but no such luck. A couple more steps and he was able to reach the bat, turning back around and swinging so hard the 1st head almost crumbled instantly like a strawberry being thrown against a wall. The second zombie had a name, Maurice already on unstable legs fell, as Hank swung and the momentum of hitting air caused him to lose his footing.

Luke was frozen staring into the mad man's eyes who had bite marks and chunks of flesh missing from his neck while his arms were reaching out for the meal to come. A flash of movement and spatter of blood to follow revealed Gary holding the other end of a crowbar. As they looked at one another, pleas from Hank could finally be heard, but once they turned their attention to the security guard and orphan, it took that quick for Hank to turn into something that was no longer alive. This time it was Gary that froze seeing people he once knew and had conversations with come at him in ways they never have before.

Luke shouted moments before impact and Gary reacted as if waking up late for work and his instincts of self-preservation kicked in along with his crowbar. He hooked Maurice in the back of the head and sending him towards Luke to swing away on and in one single motion yanking the crowbar back to stab Hank through the eye with such force the crowbar not only entered but exited out the back of his skull and simultaneously both bodies hit the ground. Another scream entered the room but this from an already on edge woman.

"AAAAAHHHHHH" Ms. Clark screamed never seeing a dead person before and never seeing someone she knew murdered with such brutality, a simple glimpse could make you lose your lunch. Gary ran to Ms. Clark to console her yet again but this was something entirely different, the world was now upside down and a sudden realization of what would become of Tim and Ms. Rodrigues, even herself sent her into a spiral of darkness that buckled her knees and sent her to the ground as lifeless as Hanks. Luke ran over to the office to tell the children and Jack it was safe to come out now...for now. When the children entered the main entrance where the bodies lie. they were all silent with eyes leaking tears from seeing familiar faces no longer familiar.

"Someone grabs some sheets and place them over their bodies and once I put Ms. Clark to bed we'll bury them outside." Said Gary now assuming the role of security as well as the groundskeeper. When no one moved he repeated himself, but more volume and this time it was Simon and the boy they called Piggy who moved together away from the crowd whispering to one another.

Luke now being free of any responsibilities went to check on the one responsibility he could never be free of. "April?" Luke said hoping to get a reply as the door creaked open. A hand peered from under the bed waving at her big brother and Luke was hit with a wave of relief. "I thought I told you to lock the door!" Luke said irritated knowing she could've been hurt.

"I heard what was going on and went into the hallway to peek through the rails and saw you hiding behind the door. When I heard the gun I ran back and under the bed. Are you okay?" asked April.

"Yea, I'm fine. I need you to stay up here a little longer. Can you do that for me?"

"Fine." April said exhaling wanting to help her big brother, and as he turned to walk out the door she asked another question. "What was wrong with that guy?"

Luke stood there not really sure himself but from the looks of what he had witnessed it was the living dead. "You know your favorite movie where they're stuck in a mall and they're zombies surrounding the place?"

"Dawn of the Dead" she answered. "Way better than the one you like."

"Night of the living dead is a classic." He said pinching her. "But seriously April, I need you to stay up here in this room. I think... they were zombies. The boy that was missing came back with bite marks and bit the security guard, and <u>then</u> he turned. Damage to the brain seems to be the only way to put them down, <u>that's</u> why I need you to stay up here." Her face showed no expression, no worry or care. A world where her parents could die why couldn't there be actual zombies. "I promise I'll be right back and well figure a way out of here." He walked out the door but not before locking it himself and entering the hallway to hear a bunch of little voices downstairs.

"I don't wanna do it, you do it!" said one of the children.

"Gary said to move them, Simon and I grabbed the blankets, least you could do is help us carry them." Said Piggy wanting to get the task over with.

"I'll help." Volunteered Luke while walking down the steps

"Course you will. Captain America over here" Jack said trying to entertain his lackeys even in the worst of situations.

"Better than hiding in an office and doing nothing." Replied Luke tired of all the big talk and wanting to see if he could back it up, but yet again they were interrupted by an adult.

"You two are the biggest here. Luke and I will grab Hank. Simon, Roger, and Jack can grab Maurice." Gary said walking back onto the scene not looking like himself, worried or hiding something. "We'll bring them out back and bury them. Willy grab us some shovels from the utility closet please and Rob, I'm going to need you to open the door for us and close it right behind us." He finished while bending down to grab a piece of the sheet that was wrapped around his deceased friend. They each lifted in unison and headed towards the back of the house and out of the door into the sunlight.

The day wasn't even close to being over and they were already burying two people and they were older. Older supposedly meant wiser but here they were about to be buried by mostly children, even though two adults remained, Ms. Clark was indisposed and Gary just didn't seem the type who could look after so many children.

"You boys keep digging. I'm going inside to check on Ms. Clark" Gary said while distributing the shovels amongst them.

The day would've been a beautiful day if not for the bloodshed. The sun was out and a light breeze to dry off any sweat that would push through the skin, even passing clouds to give breaks from the sun's rays. They all continued as they were told and even finished ahead of schedule, no thanks to Jack taking smoke breaks every 10 minutes while the others worked never saying a word to one another as if they were working it out in their own heads, but Jack didn't want to work it out on his own. "You really think Timothy infected people at the Hospital?" He asked in a sort of a worried tone but could never let go of his tough guy persona

Luke looked at Jack while patting the soil down. "It's a guess but yea I think so." Realizing Jack was actually scared for a moment. "I'm sorry for your friend." Said Luke trying to console Jack even though he truly despised him.

Jack exhaled a cloud of smoke and laughter that caused him to cough uncontrollably but the laugh could be heard through it all. "He wasn't my friend; I just don't want more of them coming this way. I'd like to stay above ground." He finished while flicking his cigarette on top of the unmarked grave.

"YOU GUYS! COME QUICK!" Yelled the little boy Rob while peeking his head out from the door and immediately slamming it shut right after.

"I wonder what's wrong." Roger said while dropping his shovel and looking up to Jack for a response.

"Bad news," Jack replied and for once, Luke and Jack were in agreement.

To Be Continued…

Printed in Great
Britain
by Amazon